written by

NYASHA WILLIAMS

illustrated by

JADE ORLANDO

ALLY BABY CAN

BE FEMINIST

HARPER

An Imprint of HarperCollinsPublishers

Who can be a feminist?

ALLY BABY CAN!

Ally Baby makes a change when they take a stand!

Being an ally is what you do
and the actions you make commonplace.

Allies **SUPPORT** those affected by inequality that is gender-based.

Societal constructs like gender will label us as *girl* or *boy*.

Sexism is discrimination against both genders, something feminism works to destroy.

PATRIARCHY
UNEQUAL
PAY
DOUBLE
STANDARDS
HARASSMENT

Ally Baby is an intersectional feminist.
For every person, they **STAND TALL**.

Ally Baby **FIGHTS** for the economic, social, and political equality of all.

YOU MATTER

Ally Baby knows a world with gender equity is best for you and me. That's why they **ADD FEMINISM** to their everyday routine.

Ally Baby **LISTENS** to others and knows when to speak up.

I've never seen a girl astronaut.

STOP! Lucia can be anything!

Ally Baby **CALLS OUT SEXISM**, even when it gets tough.

Ally Baby puts in a big effort to **LEARN**, unlearn, and accept.

Ally Baby makes mistakes but acknowledges, **APOLOGIZES**, and reflects.

Ally Baby **TAKES THEIR LEAD** from others because they value consent.

Hug, please?

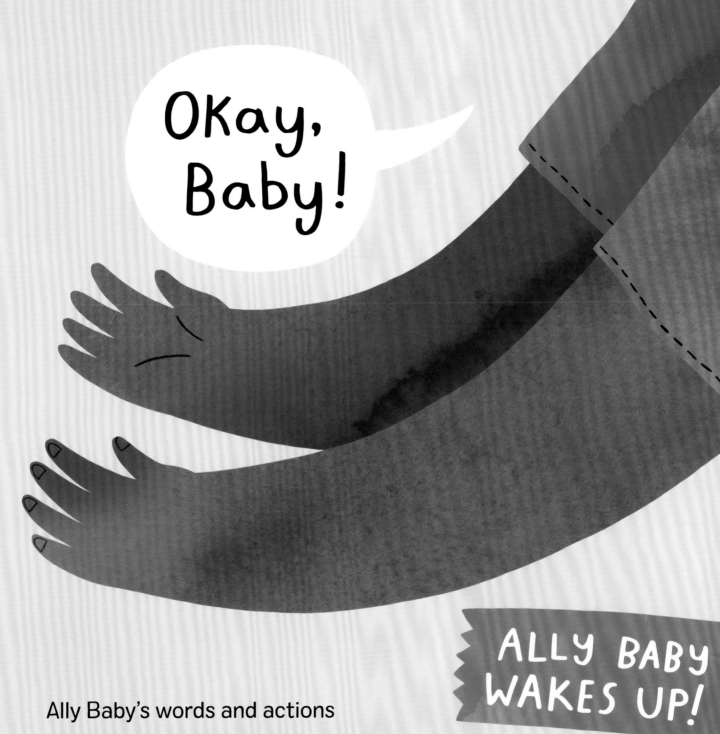

Ally Baby's words and actions always match their intent.

Ally Baby kisses Mama goodbye when maternity leave is all done.

Ally Baby **DEMANDS** more parental leave for mom, dad, and everyone.

Ally Baby **LOVES** all expressions!
All feelings are okay to feel.

TO DAY CARE!

Whether you choose to wave or smile,
Ally Baby knows *all* responses are real.

After **ADDRESSING** double standards
and right before they take a nap,

Ally Baby **ABOLISHES** the pink tax and closes the wage gap.

Ally Baby actively **BUILDS** inclusive communities.

Ally Baby fights for equal access and fair opportunities.

Ally Baby **STAYS EDUCATED** about women of yesterday and now.

Respect and **AMPLIFY** women's voices!
Ally Baby can show you how.

Ally Baby wipes the table and helps scrub the dishes clean.

Ally Baby does house and yard chores and everything in between.

Ally Baby yawns and stretches
just before they close their eyes.

GIRL
POWE

BEDTIME!

SUSIE THE
FIREFIGHTER

ALLY BABY CAN

Ally Baby **DREAMS OF POLICY CHANGE** and the day that we all rise!

Ally Baby fully commits to the ally work they do.
Ally Baby CAN be feminist and yes, friends,

SO CAN YOU!

Ally is more than a noun; it is a verb.
As an ally, you can take action against injustice when you:

ADVOCATE: Stand up in spaces where you can; use your privilege and access to resources to better serve those who are marginalized; and seize every opportunity to combat sexist ideas and dismantle sexist policy. S-u-p-p-o-r-t!

LEARN: Educate yourself, your family members, and your friends about girls' and women's experiences and about the history of sexism and gender inequality.

LET GO: Challenge your own discomforts and prejudices by letting go of sexist values. Let go of the need to be front and center; let girls and women lead too.

YIELD RESULTS: Take action to create interpersonal, societal, and institutional change.

How was Ally Baby feminist in this book?

ALLY BABY . . .

learned the definition of sex and sexism.

played with toys and wore outfits of their choice, regardless
of gender expectations.

read books and listened to the voices of marginalized women and girls.

stood up for the classmate who was told they couldn't be an astronaut
due to their gender.

apologized when they were informed that their words were
untrue and hurtful.

asked for a hug and made sure the person wanted one.

respected girls who didn't wave or smile but who, instead,
expressed how they truly felt.

made the pink and blue bottles the same price so everyone pays equally.

took responsibility for chores often left to one gender.

knows that girls can be CEOs, royalty, or anything they want to be.

What is one way you can be a feminist ally today?
How will you advocate, learn, let go, and yield results?

ALLY BABY'S FIRST WORDS

A vocabulary list for feminist allies:

ALLY: a person who is not a member of a marginalized group but who supports that group. **Coconspirator** and **advocate** are other terms often used.

AMPLIFY: to make larger and more valuable in society.

CONSENT: to ask for and to give approval, especially as it relates to one's body.

CONSTRUCT: an accepted idea that has been created by the people in a society.

DISCRIMINATION: unfair treatment of a person or group. In society, this can play out in laws, social interactions, and a nation's policy.

DOUBLE STANDARD: society's unfair acceptance of behavior from one group and not from another.

EQUITY: fairness or equality in the way people are governed and treated (also related: **social justice**, **equality**).

FEMINISM: equal and fair treatment of the sexes and all genders. **Sexism** is the opposite.

INTERSECTIONALITY: the overlap of identities that informs how an individual is treated in society. This recognizes that a white woman and an Asian trans woman have different experiences with discrimination.

PARENTAL LEAVE: paid time off for parents to raise their newborn.

In America, women have very little maternity leave and men have even less or sometimes none.

PINK TAX: unequal pricing of goods and services for girls and women.

SEX: categories of female or male based on reproductive organs and structures.
   Gender is usually assigned to us at birth. There are many genders and identities beyond the girl-boy binary.

WAGE GAP: higher pay for male employees and men than for female employees and women.

ALLY BABY'S READING LIST FOR FEMINISM

Feminist Baby by Loryn Brantz

A Is for Activist by Innosanto Nagara

Dream Big, Little One by Vashti Harrison

Shaking Things Up by Susan Hood

A Is for Awesome by Eva Chen

My First Book of Feminism by Julie Merberg

The Paper Bag Princess by Robert Munsch

Mary Wears What She Wants by Keith Negley

Ambitious Girl by Meena Harris

Grace for President by Kelly DiPucchio

Rosie Revere, Engineer by Andrea Beaty

Shady Baby by Gabrielle Union-Wade and Dwyane Wade Jr.

Good Night Stories for Rebel Girls by Elena Favilli and Francesca Cavallo

ABOUT THE CREATORS

Photo by Kimberly Salas

NYASHA WILLIAMS is an author, educator, creator, and activist who works to decolonize literature, minds, and spiritual practices one day at a time. She is the author of the picture books *What's the Commotion in the Ocean?* and *I Affirm Me.* You can visit her at www.nyashawilliams.online.

Photo by Raven Shutley Studios

JADE ORLANDO was born on an army base in North Carolina and grew up in a tiny Michigan town. She is the illustrator of several works for children, including *Hey You!*, *Generation Brave*, and *Who Takes Care of You?* Jade currently lives in Atlanta, GA, with her husband, greyhound, and four cats (including two naked ones!). You can visit her at www.jadefrolics.com.

Ally Baby Can: Be Feminist • Copyright © 2022 by HarperCollins Publishers • Written by Nyasha Williams • Illustrated by Jade Orlando • Special thanks to **Little Feminist** for their authenticity read, and to Luana Kay Horry • All rights reserved • Manufactured in Italy • No part of this book may be used or reproduced in any manner whatsoever without written permission except in the case of brief quotations embodied in critical articles and reviews • For information address HarperCollins Children's Books, a division of HarperCollins Publishers, 195 Broadway, New York, NY 10007 • www.harpercollinschildrens.com • Library of Congress Control Number: 2021948583 • ISBN 978-0-06-321454-5 The artist used watercolor, Adobe Photoshop, and Procreate to create the digital illustrations for this book • Typography by Caitlin Stamper
22 23 24 25 26 RTLO 10 9 8 7 6 5 4 3 2 1 ❖ First Edition